The

Boggy Bay
Marathon

Other Orchard Storybooks

Clipper Street Stories by Bernard Ashley
CALLING FOR SAM
TALLER THAN BEFORE

Jupiter Jane Stories by Sheila Lavelle
THE APPLE PIE ALIEN

Woodside School Stories by Jean Ure
THE FRIGHT
WHO'S TALKING?

A JUPITER JANE STORY

The
Boggy Bay
Marathon

Sheila Lavelle

Illustrated by
Emma Crosby

ORCHARD BOOKS
London

First published in Great Britain in 1987 by
ORCHARD BOOKS
10 Golden Square, London W1R 3AF
Orchard Books Australia
14 Mars Road, Lane Cove NSW 2066
Orchard Books Canada
20 Torbay Road, Markham, Ontario 23P 1G6
1 85213 082 2
Printed in Great Britain
by A. Wheaton, Exeter

I

Katy Stuart opened her eyes one drizzly morning in August with that nasty sinking feeling in her stomach. The one you get when it's spelling-test day, or you're going into hospital to have your tonsils out. Something awful was going to happen today, but for the moment Katy couldn't remember what.

She burrowed under the blankets and tried to go back to sleep, but music was coming from the other bed in Katy's room. Jupiter Jane was playing her tinkle-board again, and the tune made Katy twitch all

5

over. She groaned and pulled the covers off her head.

"Shut up, Jane," she said crossly. "I'm still asleep."

The girl in the next bed scowled. "You're talking in your sleep, then, Grumpy-pants," she said. But she stopped playing the tinkle-board, a guitar-like instrument with thirteen strings and rows of tiny silver bells, and sent it floating away across the room to the large metal box she'd brought in her spaceship from Jupiter.

"That was a special wake-up tune," she said, jumping across onto Katy's bed and bouncing about on it as if it were a trampoline. "We're going to your grandmother's today, don't forget, and your mum wants an early start."

Katy groaned. The day she had been dreading was here at last. She was very fond of her grandma, but she didn't half have some peculiar ideas. Visiting her at Boggy Bay for a holiday was bad enough, without having to take an alien from space along as well. If only her dad hadn't answered that advertisement in the newspaper, Katy thought, none of this would have happened.

'Family wanted to take care of

young female visitor from the planet Jupiter,' it had said, and Mr Stuart had been too curious for his own good. Jupiter Jane had arrived, in her own two-seater spaceship, and nothing had been the same since.

Katy had become used to Jane's orange webbed feet by now. She had even got used to her habit of sending things flying through the air using nothing but the force of her own will-power. But what she couldn't get used to was the way Jane tried to boss everybody about, and the annoying way she sniggered at everything she saw, calling all Earth things old-fashioned, and writing notes about them in a blue notebook she kept in her pocket.

Worst of all, the family hadn't

been able to get rid of their guest at the end of her two-week visit, for the solar-powered spaceship was unable to take off in bad weather, and this was turning out to be the wettest summer since the time of Noah's Ark. Now they were making their annual trip to Gran's, and they had no choice but to take their visitor with them. There was nothing they could do about it except pray that Jane would behave herself, but Katy didn't have much hope of that.

"You'd better wear your boots today, Jane," said Katy, slipping out of bed. "We don't want my Gran to see your feet. She might have a heart attack."

"Knickers to that," said Jane scornfully, pulling blue dungarees up over her plate-sized webbed feet that made her one of the world's fastest swimmers. "Gran will have to see my feet some time, won't she? So it may as well be today." And off she waddled to the bath-room for her morning paddle.

Katy dressed quickly and ran downstairs to the kitchen, where her mum stood guard over scrambled eggs on the stove, her head bristling with spiked curlers like a new kind of deadly weapon. Katy's dad was outside, stuffing bags and suitcases into the car, and looking flustered from trying to fit ten cubic metres of luggage into two cubic metres of space.

"You needn't bother packing those golf clubs, Charlie," his wife shouted at him through the open doorway. "You won't be going off on your own to enjoy yourself, you know." She slashed fiercely at a loaf of bread with the breadknife as if it was trying to escape.

Mr Stuart took no notice. He shoved his golf bag into the car, removing his wife's bulky parcel of knitting to make room for it, and spilling balls of coloured wool all over the gravel. Katy ran out to help him.

"Cheer up, Dad," she said, giving him a hug. "Maybe it won't be so bad this time."

Katy's dad made a long sad face like a sick goldfish. "It'll be worse," he said gloomily, pushing his glasses back on his nose. "Gran's been on one of those keep fit courses. We'll have to jog ten miles every morning before breakfast this time, instead of just five. And I bet she's entered us for the Boggy Bay Sponsored Sports again."

His wife came out to put a packet of sandwiches into the car. "It won't do you any harm," she said shortly. "It might even get some of that fat off you. You've got a belly like a beach ball."

An hour later they were ready to leave. Somehow room had been found for everything in the car, including Jane's tinkle-board which she refused to be parted from. Tommy the cat had been sent off to his favourite neighbour, the geraniums had been watered, and the small silver spaceship had been safely locked in the garage.

"Right, everybody," said Katy's dad glumly, looking as if he were on his way to the dentist rather than a week's holiday. "Let's go." The girls scrambled into the back seat and the car leapt forward and rattled down the driveway towards the street.

"Blast!" muttered Katy's dad, for their exit was blocked by the milk float which was parked in the road. As usual, Mr Stuart's normal placid nature had vanished as soon as he got behind the wheel of the car, and he tooted the horn and revved the engine impatiently.

"He'll be having coffee with that Mrs Murphy again," tutted Mrs Stuart, when the milkman did not return. "He could be there for hours."

Jane was staring disgustedly at the stacks of crates. "That's a stupid way to get your milk," she said. "On Jupiter every family keeps a goat. My dad has to milk ours every morning before he makes my mum's breakfast."

She suddenly scrambled out of the car and marched into the road. While the family watched, round-eyed, she pointed the fingers of her right hand straight at the milk float.

"I don't believe it," said Mr Stuart faintly, as the milk float rocked slightly and rose a little way off the ground. Then, bottles clinking gently, it sailed steadily along the street and round the corner.

Katy's mum, speechless for once, gaped at the space where it had been.

"I'd love to see the milkman's face when he comes out," said Katy, as Jane climbed triumphantly in beside her.

"Let's get moving before he does," muttered Katy's dad, putting the gears into reverse by mistake and swearing as they shot backwards up the drive. Finally the car lurched out into the street and roared up the hill towards the motorway, with Jane gazing eagerly out of the window, her notebook at the ready.

2

A thin, white-haired lady in running shoes and a pink tracksuit that made her look like an elderly flamingo opened the door of the cottage. She beamed at them as they stood on the doorstep in the rain.

"Katy!" she cried. "How lovely to see you!"

Katy was feeling worn out from the journey and from the strain of answering Jane's never-ending questions about the farms, the tractors, the crops, the animals, the birds, the rivers, the roads, the traffic, the trees, and a thousand and one other things. She shut her eyes as Gran lifted her off the ground in a hard, bony hug.

Gran put Katy down and turned to Mrs Stuart. "You too, Maggie dear. And Charles!"

"I'll get the luggage," said Mr Stuart hastily, escaping round the corner, and knocking a potted petunia off the window-sill in his hurry.

"This must be your friend from Jupiter," Katy's grandma went on, shaking Jane violently by the hand. "My word, I do like those flippers. Wish I had feet like that. I wouldn't half show the old bats at the swimming club something then."

Katy sighed with relief. Gran wasn't at all put out by those orange feet, and it looked as though she might be prepared to get on with their visitor after all. Now it all depended on Jane. Katy waited anxiously for her first words, expecting the usual rude reply. But a most extraordinary thing happened.

"It's an honour to meet you, your ladyship," said Jane and she bowed low three times.

Everybody stared in amazement, and Katy had to bite her hanky to stop herself from laughing out loud.

"Stand up, Jane, you foolish girl," said Katy's mum, giving her a shake. "There's no need for that. It's only Katy's gran."

Jane glared at her in disgust. "What's wrong?" she said. "Don't you treat your grandmothers with respect on this stupid planet? I'd better make a note of that." She took her notebook from her pocket.

"On Jupiter they're in charge of everything," she said, as they stepped into the hall, which was filled with a strange smell as if someone were boiling a very old cabbage. Katy almost choked, but Jane didn't seem to notice. "We have the Honourable Council of Grandmothers," she went on, "who run the planet and make the laws and things. And everybody respects them, because they are old and wise. Isn't it like that here?"

Katy's grandma gave a snort that made her false teeth rattle. "Not a bit," she said cheerfully. "The youngsters run things here. We oldies do just as we please, and that's the way we like it."

She pulled a pink sweat-band down over her brow. "Come along, you lot," she ordered. "What you need now is exercise. We've just got time to run a mile or two along the beach before that lovely nettle soup is ready." She sprinted away through the puddles on the garden path.

Some time later the family sat down to bowls of something hot and green and slimy. Katy and her dad looked at one another in dismay, while Mrs Stuart tasted hers in grim silence. Jane, who had opted for a swim in the sea instead of a run, attacked the food hungrily.

"This is really great, your ladyship," she said, dipping chunks of home-made wholewheat concrete into her bowl. "It's just like my dad makes back home on Jupiter. And he's a very good cook." She

smiled round at them all proudly.

Katy's grandma was serving the next course, a dish of lentilburgers and black beans.

"Glad you like it," she said, adding portions of a wrinkled grey fungus that she had collected in the woods, and not noticing Mr Stuart pouring his soup into a potted fern. "It's full of natural goodness. Much better for you than hamburgers and ice-cream and all that rubbish. It'll build you up for the Boggy Bay Sponsored Sports next Saturday. I've put your names down for the five-mile marathon."

Katy's heart sank into her sandals. She hated all kinds of sport except Ludo, and running was the worst sport of all.

Her dad groaned, his mouth full of beans. "I don't think my knees will stand up to the marathon this year, Gran," he spluttered, wiping his steamed-up glasses on his Snoopy T-shirt. "I'll just go fishing instead."

"Rubbish," said Gran. "The whole family will run as usual. Jane as well, of course."

"What's a marathon?" asked Jane, looking up from her plate. Her eyes widened as Katy's grandma explained.

"I can't run," she protested at once. "There's not much land on Jupiter, you see. It's mostly water."

She slipped down from her chair and flapped awkwardly around the floor. "Look at these feet, your ladyship," she said. "They're great for swimming, and even walking. But they're not much use for running a five-mile marathon, are they?"

Katy held her breath. Nobody ever argued with Grandma. It just wasn't done. Gran gazed round at them all as if she couldn't believe her ears. There was a small silence.

"I suppose you're right," she said grudgingly at last, and everybody breathed again. "I'll enter you for the swimming event instead. But there's no excuse for the rest of you. I've already put your names down. We'll raise a lot of money for charity if we complete the course."

"What's charity?" asked Jane eagerly, grabbing her notebook, but Katy's gran had disappeared into the kitchen to avoid any more arguments. Katy saw her dad sink down in his chair, and not another word did he say for the rest of the meal.

"You can stop hiding that stuff under the cushions and get it eaten up," Mrs Stuart told him, as soon as Gran was out of the room. Katy's dad poked about in his seat, fished out a few pieces of the leathery fungus, and flung them outside into the garden.

"Feeding the birds?" beamed Gran, coming back with one of her

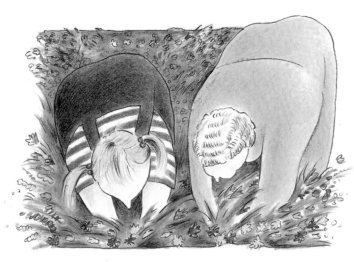

unsweetened rhubarb pies that took the skin off your teeth. "That's nice. Now come and have your lovely pudding. I've got some little jobs for you after dinner."

Katy helped her mother with the washing-up, while Jane went with Gran on a tour of the garden, collecting seeds and cuttings to take back to Jupiter, and making notes about Earth's vegetables and herbs. The rain had stopped, so Mr Stuart was set to work mending a garden wall.

"I hope you're not mixing cement in your best trousers," his wife shouted at him through the open window.

"Of course not," he shouted back. "I'm using a bucket." He winked at Katy when she burst out laughing.

"Never mind, Dad," she said to him at bedtime, as the family slowly climbed the stairs, after mugs of dandelion tea and biscuits that would crack the teeth of a Doberman. "Only six more days to go."

"I don't think I'll last that long," said Mr Stuart, limping along the landing. "Gran wants us up at six in the morning to start training for the marathon."

"You'll survive," said his wife sourly. "It's not you I'm worried about. It's Gran." She leaned tiredly against the stair rail. "I know she's fit, but all this can't really be good for her at her age."

Jane nodded her head worriedly. "Her ladyship should get more rest," she said. "I think I know a little trick that will help her."

Katy's mum gave Jane a disapproving look. "Just leave Grandma alone," she said. "We don't want any of your crazy tricks here, my girl."

Jane merely smiled as she went along the landing to their room, but Katy knew by the gleam in her eyes that something was going to happen very soon.

33

3

Next morning dawned grey and chilly, and in spite of their protests Katy's family had to start the day at six o'clock with a jog along the beach before breakfast, followed by a dip in the cold North Sea.

"Come along, don't lag!" shouted Gran. "You'll never be fit for the marathon at this rate." Katy, who couldn't swim, struggled along at the edge of the water, watching enviously as Jane's blue swimsuit and orange feet flashed in and out of the waves with no trouble at all.

After breakfast, a choice between

watery porridge and granite toast with crab-apple jelly, the morning continued with chores around the cottage and garden. Mr Stuart was set the task of building a garden shed, a job which kept him busy for hours since it fell down as many times as he put it up.

Jane, after her daily practice on her tinkle-board, pottered about the vegetable patch, tending the rows of spinach and beans, exclaiming in delight over every creepy-crawly she found, and helping Katy's grandma to spread steaming barrowloads of horse manure. She laughed until she almost choked when she learnt what the stuff was, jotting it down gleefully in her notebook and shaking her head in amazement. Katy noticed that from time to time she kept going off into a corner and humming to herself, as if trying to remember a forgotten piece of music.

Katy's grandma never bothered her head about housework, so Mrs Stuart and Katy, in overalls and with scarves tied around their hair, spent a few hours giving the cottage its annual summer clean-up. A huge black spider was ejected from his home under the piano and released over the garden wall, after a lot of argument with Jane who wanted to keep him for a pet.

"What's wrong with him?" she demanded, when Katy squealed and shuddered. "He's much nicer than your horrible cat. Everybody keeps spiders on Jupiter. They're cute." It was only at Gran's insistence that she gave in and let him go, much to Katy's relief.

A salad of dandelion leaves and cold chickpeas was Gran's idea of an early lunchtime snack, after which came a six-mile hike into the hills behind the village. Gran strode out in her walking boots, woollen socks and baggy shorts, and there was trouble for anyone who dared suggest stopping for a rest.

"Come along, keep moving," she roared, as Katy's dad lingered wistfully near the doorway of the village pub. "We've still got another five miles to go."

Mr Stuart heaved a sigh. "I'd give anything for a pint," he told the others, while Gran was still too far ahead to hear. "And a big, juicy steak. With fried onions and mustard. Some of the stuff that's bad for you for a change."

"Or a toasted cheese-burger," Katy said longingly, her hair sticking up like a haystack in the wind. "Or barbecued sausages with tomato sauce."

"Or a slice of Mrs Stuart's apple pie," said Jane, plodding along in her big rubber boots. "Life's not the same without it." The family gazed after her in surprise as she hurried away to catch up with Gran.

Later that evening they all gathered in the sitting-room after a meal of lettuce leaves stuffed with brown rice and spinach. Katy's stomach rumbled hungrily since she'd followed her dad's example and scraped most of it out of the window while her grandma was busy in the kitchen.

"A little rest before we begin the evening chores," smiled Gran, sitting next to Katy on the sofa. "Look, the sun's coming out at last. We can do some more work in the garden. Jane's very good at spreading manure, you know. She doesn't even need a pitchfork. It seems to fly around all by itself."

"It smells like Pooh Corner out there," giggled Katy. Her dad snorted with laughter, and Mrs

Stuart gave them both a sour look as if she'd swallowed a spoonful of nasty medicine.

Jane wrote 'Pooh Corner' carefully in her notebook. Then she sat on a stool near the window, her tinkle-board across her knees. "Would you like to hear some music, your ladyship?" she said.

"That would be nice," agreed Gran, leaning against the cushions. Jane bent her head and began to pluck the strings and tap the tiny silver bells. Music filled the room, soft, gentle and strangely compelling. A feeling of warmth and peace crept over Katy from the tips of her toes to the top of her head and she had to struggle to keep her eyes open. She glanced at her mum and dad, who both had their eyes shut fast. Then a faint sound made her turn her head to look at Gran.

Katy's grandma had slumped down into a corner of the sofa, her eyes tightly closed, and her mouth wide open as if she were at the dentist for a filling. She was snoring steadily.

"Good. That's done the trick," whispered Jane, laying the tinkle-board aside. "It's a lullaby we use on Jupiter to put babies to sleep at night. I've been trying to get it right all day." She padded softly towards the door. "Wake your parents, Katy. We can all go down to the village. I'm going to have the biggest piece of apple pie they've got." She slipped away upstairs to put on her boots.

Katy wasted no time. She shook her mother gently by the shoulder, then her dad. They came awake slowly, blinking and staring around them in a bewildered sort of way.

"Don't let me wake up," moaned Katy's dad. "I dreamt I was in a pub. I had this great foaming tankard in my hand…"

"Ssh!" hissed Katy, as her mother rubbed her eyes and groaned.

"Don't wake Grandma. We're all going out."

They both stared at Gran, fast asleep on the sofa.

"Good lord," breathed Katy's dad. "How long will she stay like that?"

"All night, if you don't wake her," said Jane, standing in the doorway in her boots. "And when she wakes up she won't even remember that she's been asleep. Come on, everybody, let's go."

Katy's mum looked doubtful. "I don't like it," she said. "Are you sure she'll be all right?"

Mr Stuart lifted Gran's feet onto the cushions and covered her with a rug. "Of course she will," he said. "A long rest will do her the world of good." He took his wife by the elbow and steered her towards the door. "Come along, Maggie. I'll buy you a decent cup of tea."

Mrs Stuart didn't need any more persuading. With a last look at Gran they all crept out of the house and down the path, like truants sneaking out of school.

4

Saturday brought a fine day for the Boggy Bay Sports and the sun came out for the first time since April. Katy's grandma, in her new yellow jogging suit and Nike shoes, beamed at the family as they trooped downstairs for breakfast.

"How do I look?" she said, turning round to let them see.

"Lovely," said Jane. "Just like a banana."

"You'll be the best grandma in the marathon," said Katy, wishing that marathons had never been invented.

"You'll be the only grandma in the marathon," said Katy's mum tartly. "All the others have got more sense." She sat down and poured out a cup of raspberry-leaf tea, frowning at her husband who was having a practice jog around the dining-room in his shorts.

"Well, Gran," he said, spreading stewed green gooseberries on his toast, "it's our last day. And I think we all agree it's been the best holiday we've ever had at Boggy Bay."

He grinned at Katy as he said it, and Katy smiled back weakly. If it wasn't for the dreaded marathon still to come, it wouldn't have been a bad holiday at all. Thanks to the magic music of the tinkle-board, it had been a simple matter to send

Gran off to sleep whenever they felt like escaping, and as she never remembered anything about it afterwards, the family had been able to do as they pleased for much of the time.

Katy's dad had played a few games of golf and hired a boat for an afternoon's fishing. A keen bargain-hunter, Mrs Stuart had driven into Newcastle to wander around the department stores and complain about the prices. Katy had seen very little of Jane who had spent all her time on the beach exploring the rock pools, armed with Gran's copy of *The Naturelover's Guide to the Seashore*.

It had been bliss for Katy, who liked nothing better than to laze around reading, dozing and listening to the radio. She had put all thoughts of the marathon out of her head, and had even climbed up the hill behind the village with her watercolour paintbox, to paint a picture of Boggy Bay that even Jane had admired.

Every evening they all sneaked off to the village inn, to stuff themselves with steak and ice-cream. Mr Stuart's first pint of beer had gone down so fast it hadn't even touched the sides, and Jane had eaten seven portions of apple pie before she'd had enough.

"I'm glad you've had a nice time," said Gran, serving bowls of lumpy grey porridge. "You're all looking very well, I must say. And it's done me the world of good having you here, you know. I feel surprisingly rested. I can't think why." Katy had to jump up and bang her dad on the back as he choked on his mouthful of toast.

The Boggy Bay Sponsored Sports was the event of the year, and the village was already crowded when the family walked down to the beach later that morning. Flags and bunting decorated every street and lamp-post, stalls were being set up on the pavements and along the harbour walls, and a brass band was rehearsing for the afternoon's concert.

"Are you nervous?" Katy asked Jane as they arrived at the open-air swimming pool, where a large crowd had already gathered to watch the sponsored swim.

Jane tossed her pigtails in disdain. "Nervous? Me?" she said. "Don't be ridiculous."

"All swimmers this way," called a fat, bald man with a bushy black beard that made him look as if he had his head on upside down. "Starting-gun goes in five minutes." He began collecting entry forms and ticking off the names of the competitors on his clipboard.

Leaving her boots, sweatshirt and jeans with Katy, Jane pushed her way through the spectators to the edge of the pool, ignoring the stares and whispers as people nudged one another and pointed at her huge webbed feet.

"Good luck, Jane," Katy called after her, before following her family up the steps towards the rows of seats. It was some time before they found four seats together, but they sat down at last, only to find some sort of argument going on at the pool's edge. Katy groaned when she saw that a small figure in a blue swimsuit seemed to be at the centre of it all.

The fat man with the beard was waving his clipboard about and shouting at Jane.

"No flippers allowed in the pool!" he bellowed, pointing to a large sign. "Don't you understand? Take them off, girl!"

Jane, hands on hips and chin stuck out defiantly, was shouting straight back.

"I can't take them off, you silly little man," she yelled. "They're not flippers, they're my FEET!"

The crowd, loving every minute of it, cheered and stamped and whistled. The fat man, tugging at his beard in exasperation, looked round for help. A lady official tried to reason with Jane, but with no effect. She stood stubbornly on the starting line, while the other swimmers, chilled by the delay, jumped up and down to try to keep warm.

"I'd better to do something," said Katy's dad, getting up hastily and knocking a straw hat off a man's head in the next row. "Oops, sorry, madam," he stammered, making matters worse by snatching up the hat and shoving it back on the wrong head before rushing off down the steps.

"Wait for me," called Gran, jumping up and hurrying after him.

The argument by the pool had now reached a full-scale row, with several of the organisers bawling at one another and waving their arms. Then Katy held her breath as two more figures appeared on the scene. Gran only added to the confusion by pulling at Jane's feet in an attempt to prove that they really couldn't come off, and Katy's dad did nothing at all except get in everybody's way. Finally two large ladies in tracksuits grabbed Jane's elbows and attempted to lead her away from the pool.

"Disqualified!" declared the fat man, turning his back on Katy's furious grandma. "Disqualified for attempting to cheat!" He scribbled on his list of entries, while the crowd hissed and booed as if it were a pantomime.

What happened next could have been an accident. Katy never really found out whether it was, but she kept her suspicions to herself.

The two large ladies holding Jane's arms suddenly let go and leapt into the air as if they had been stung. They clung together for a moment, teetering on the edge of the pool, before falling into the water with a splash.

The spectators roared with delight, then roared again when the first splash was followed by an even

bigger one as the fat man also fell in for no reason at all. Jane turned and stomped furiously away, appearing a few moments later at Katy's side, her face covered in scowls.

"You haven't half got some funny people on this planet," she muttered sulkily. "They're even stupider than the Martians, and that's saying something."

"Get dressed, Jane," said Katy's dad, coming back at the same time. "Let's get out of here." The crowd was too busy watching the officials being fished out of the pool to notice them leave.

Gran met them at the bottom of the steps as they made their escape. She looked hopping mad.

"I've never been so insulted in my life," she fumed. "Accused of cheating! At my age! That's what you get from helping people with their wretched charities." She took the family's entry forms out of her pocket, tore them into shreds, and flung the bits away into the wind.

"They can keep their marathon in future," she declared. "This is one family who won't be running any more."

Gran put her arm round Jane, whose sulks were disappearing fast. "Come on, Jane, let's forget all about their silly sports. We'll all go home for a nice cup of dandelion coffee." Off they marched together up the lane, leaving Katy and her parents standing speechless on the pavement.

Katy's dad recovered first. He took both Katy's hands and they danced a jig in the street.

"No marathon!" shouted Katy. After dreading it all this time it seemed too good to be true.

"We'll all go fishing instead,"

said her dad gleefully.

"You'll do no such thing," glowered Katy's mum, sucking in her cheeks as if she'd swallowed a mouthful of dishwater. "You can both help me with the packing. We're going home tomorrow, don't forget."

Katy could hardly believe her luck. No horrible marathon, and Gran was so mad that she probably wouldn't enter them next year, either. Or ever again, come to that. Holidays at Boggy Bay might not be so bad in future, after all.

As Katy stood there in the sunshine another thought struck her. The weather was improving, and Jane's spaceship would be able to take off before very long. They could get rid of their visitor, and life could get back to normal at last.

Katy's feet hardly touched the ground as she linked arms with her dad and followed the others back to the cottage.